To Denise,
for all her help with this book

First U.S. edition 2004

Library of Congress Cataloging-in-Publication Data

Browne, Anthony, date.
Into the forest / Anthony Browne. —1st U.S. ed.
p. cm.
Summary: After his father seems to disappear, a boy takes a cake to his ill grandmother,
traveling through the forest in a journey reminiscent of the story of Little Red Riding Hood.
ISBN 0-7636-2511-6
[1. Adventure and adventurers—Fiction. 2. Grandmother—Fiction. 3. Fathers and sons—Fiction.] I. Title.
PZ7.B81984In 2004
[E]—dc22   2003069576

2 4 6 8 10 9 7 5 3 1

Printed in China

This book was typeset in Poliphilus MT.
The illustrations were done in pencil and watercolor.

Candlewick Press
2067 Massachusetts Avenue
Cambridge, Massachusetts 02140

visit us at www.candlewick.com

Into the Forest

Anthony Browne

CANDLEWICK PRESS
CAMBRIDGE, MASSACHUSETTS

One night I was wakened by a terrible sound.

The next morning all was quiet. Dad wasn't there. I asked Mom when he was coming back, but she didn't seem to know.

I missed Dad.

The next day Mom asked me to take a cake to Grandma, who was not feeling well. I love Grandma. She always tells me such fantastic stories. There are two ways to get to Grandma's house: the long way around, which takes a long time, or the short way through the forest.

"Don't go into the forest," said Mom. "Go the long way around."

But that day, for the
first time, I chose the quick
way. I wanted to be home
in case Dad came back.

After a short while I saw a boy.

"Do you want to buy a nice milky moo-cow?" he asked.

"No," I said. (Why would I want a cow?)

"I'll swap it for that sweet fruity-cake in your basket," he said.

"No, it's for my sick grandma," I said, and walked on.

"*I'm* sick," I heard him saying. "*I'm* sick. . . ."

As I went farther into the forest, I met a girl with golden hair.

"What a sweet little basket," she said. "What's in it?"

"A cake for my grandma. She's sick."

"*I'd* like a nice cake like that," she said.

I walked on and could hear her saying, "But it's a nice little cake. *I'd* like one like that. . . ."

The forest was becoming darker and colder, and I saw two other children huddling by a fire.

"Have you seen our dad and mom?" the boy asked.

"No, have you lost them?"

"They're cutting wood in the forest somewhere," said the girl, "but I wish they'd come back."

As I walked on, I could hear the dreadful sound of the girl crying, but what could I do?

I was getting very cold and wished that I'd brought a coat.

Suddenly I saw one. It was nice and warm, but as soon as I put

it on, I began to feel scared. I felt that something was following me.

I remembered a story that Grandma used to tell me about a bad wolf.

I started to run, but I couldn't find the path. I ran and ran, deeper

into the forest, but I was lost. Where was Grandma's house?

At last—there it was!

I knocked on the door and a voice called out, "Who's there?" But it didn't really sound like Grandma's voice.

"It's me. I've brought a cake from Mom." I pushed the door open a little.

"Come in, dear," the strange voice called.

I was terrified. I slowly crept in. There in Grandma's bed was . . .

Grandma!

"Come here, love," she sniffed. "How are you?"

"I'm all right now," I said.

Then I heard a noise behind me and turned around . . .

DAD!

I told them everything that had happened. We all had a
hot drink, and I ate two pieces of Mom's delicious cake. Then
we said goodbye to Grandma, who was feeling much better.

When we got home, I pushed open the door.

"Who's there?" a voice called.

"It's only us," we said.

And Mom came out smiling.